THE OUTFIT #3

KIDNAP AT DENTON FARM

Robert Swindells

ISBN 978-1-78270-055-5

Illustrations by Leo Hartas

First published by Scholastic Ltd 1993
This edition published by Award Publications Limited 2014

Published by Award Publications Limited,
The Old Riding School, The Welbeck Estate,
Worksop, Nottinghamshire, S80 3LR

www.awardpublications.co.uk

14 1

Printed in the United Kingdom